ONE FINE NIGHT

SPECIAL OPS SCOTS PREQUEL

KAIT NOLAN

TAKE THE LEAP PUBLISHING

1

ALEX

Sentinel: Is it done?

I stared at the text message for a long moment before thumbing back a reply.

Me: Aye. It's done.

Actually telling someone who knew me, knew my situation—or most of it—made the weight of this new reality settle on my shoulders. I couldn't say it was comfortable. Maybe it wasn't supposed to be.

Sentinel: How do you feel?

As if I had a ready answer for that? My thumbs hovered over the screen for a long moment as I struggled to find something to say. My skin felt too tight. Every inch prickled with awareness of the droves of people moving about King's Cross, boarding and debarking from trains. I'd tucked myself into a corner, out of the flow of pedestrian traffic, with two points of egress and a clear view of the board listing train platforms and statuses. Not that I thought I'd need an escape route. Probably. But my training was too hard to break.

I automatically assessed the people walking past me. The thirty-something career woman with the confident strut and a mobile phone at her ear. The blokes in rugby kit on their way to a match in Manchester, gear bags thrown over their shoulders. The guy with a watchful gaze I pegged as off-duty law enforcement. The harried mum with a toddler on her hip racing for the train to Cardiff. The middle-aged businessman escorting his aging mum and frustrated with it.

It was instinct to categorize their potential threat level. Habit to make note of every exit and potential source of weapons. Not that I needed any. I'd been trained to be plenty deadly with nothing but my bare hands.

A massive *BOOM* shook the building.

Instantly, I dropped behind a nearby rubbish bin for cover as startled pedestrians screamed.

What the bloody hell?

I scanned the station, searching for smoke and flames and carnage.

Finding none, my pulse ratcheted up further as I frantically tried to assess the threat without sufficient data.

"Sorry! Sorry!"

I spotted a hubbub around one of the platforms further down. It had been cordoned off for construction. I realized a cable had snapped, and a steel girder had fallen from the arm of a crane. Not too far, thankfully, and it seemed no one had been injured.

There was no bomb. No threat. At least, not the sort I was accustomed to handling.

The dozens of curious glances sent my way proved I'd taken longer to clue into that than the other travelers in the station. More than a little self-conscious, I rose to my feet, not meeting anyone's gaze, lest the eye contact invite conversation.

At least I had an answer for my former section leader now.

Picking up the phone I'd dropped, I tapped out a reply.

> Me: Ill equipped to be a civilian.

My heart rate had slowed by the time the three dots began to bounce, signaling a response.

> Sentinel: It gets better. Give it time.

Time. Aye. Right. I had plenty of that now that I was done with the Royal Marines. I knew what I was supposed to do—find new connections to replace the community and family I'd had in the military. Work. A purpose. A safety net. And ultimately, relationships that would help make up for the loss of my section.

Not that I could imagine anything taking the place of that brotherhood. We'd fought and bled together. Seen things that would cow lesser men. Things that made my reaction entirely reasonable instead of outsized.

Maybe when I wasn't devoting all this energy to threat assessment, those tasks wouldn't feel so bloody overwhelming.

How long would that take?

For the hundredth time since I'd signed the last of the paperwork, I questioned my decision. This was years earlier than I'd planned to retire. But under the circumstances, it had seemed the best course of action.

Glancing back up at the departure board, I saw my train was finally boarding. Shoving my phone into a pocket, I shouldered my pack and made my way to the proper platform. By tonight, I'd be back in the Highlands, spending some time with my section leader, who'd made this transition himself two years ago. I hoped the trip would give me clarity and a better foundation for how the hell to navigate this unfamiliar civilian world.

Most of the passengers from the previous service had disembarked by the time I slipped onto the train, so I had my choice of seats. Choosing one at the front of the car, I dumped my bag into the seat beside the window and sat on the aisle, facing the rest of the car. I stretched out my long legs without apology, hoping no one would attempt to sit in the row across from me. I didn't want to be that close to anyone I didn't know. Didn't want to be forced to make casual conversation.

Evidently the don't-mess-with-me vibes I was projecting worked because no one tried to encroach upon my space as the train car began to fill. My fingers drummed restlessly against my leg, an unpardonable tell. I wished for my laptop and all the technological bells and whistles that would've enabled me to put together dossiers on every single person in this car. It was the sort of thing I'd do for mission prep.

But civilians didn't live their life with that kind of intel. So I twitched and tried to ignore the tightening of my chest as more and more people boarded.

"—och, no. You wouldn't believe the crap the organizers passed on to me."

At the Scots accent that reminded me of home, my fingers stopped tapping, and I zeroed in on the woman who'd just walked past my seat. Long, dark brown hair fell past her shoulders. I pegged her as maybe 5' 7" or 8", with willowy legs carrying her down the aisle. A backpack was slung over one shoulder, and she pushed one of those four-wheeled rolling suitcases in front of her, holding her mobile to her ear with one hitched shoulder.

"Aye, I should be back by then. Drinks at T and B? Say around seven?"

The person on the other end of the phone replied, and a peal of female laughter carried back to where I sat. The sound of that laugh struck me in the chest, loosening the band that had progressively tightened with each person who'd entered the space.

The woman chose a seat several rows back.

"Hey, I need to go. I'm on the train, and I don't want to be one of *those* people. But I'll see you tonight, aye? Right. See you there." She tucked the phone into the back pocket of dark jeans that cupped her very fine arse, then lifted the suitcase to the rack above the seats. She had to stretch to do it, showing off long, lean limbs and a swatch of creamy skin where her shirt rode up.

I had the most absurd urge to touch that skin, to see if it was as soft as it looked.

She settled into a seat facing the front, and I got my first look at her face.

Utterly gorgeous.

Younger than I'd realized, too. Early twenties, with an oval face, high cheekbones, and bright blue eyes that I could see even from where I sat several rows away. Eyes that weren't laughing as she had been on the phone call, but instead held worry. With a deep sigh, her shoulders slumped and her head bowed, her hair swinging forward to hide those eyes. Everything in her posture said she'd just been putting on a show for whoever had been on the phone.

I wanted to know what was wrong and how I could help fix it.

Which was utterly ridiculous. I didn't know this woman. She was a stranger on a train. The likelihood that anything going on with her was within my ability to help seemed slim. But it didn't change the itch to do... something.

Was she traveling alone? So far as I could tell, no one was sitting with her. She'd barely done more than glance and smile at the woman in the seat opposite her. Was Inverness her final destination, as mine was? Or would she be getting off at one of the stops along the way?

It didn't matter. The fleeting sort of connection I might make here wasn't what I needed to focus on. There was the matter of what the hell I was going to do with the rest of my life.

The conductor announced the doors were closing, and I settled back into my seat.

At least I'd have something lovely to look at for part of the trip.

2

CIARA

I stared at my laptop screen, realizing I'd been rereading the same two lines for at least the past thirty minutes. I had hours more before I got home, and I'd planned to use this time to get some work done on my capstone project. But I was too much in my head and couldn't focus, even with the comforting and familiar rhythmic thump of the tracks beneath me.

A strident voice pulled my attention across the aisle, where a pinch-faced woman glared at her companion. I had no idea what she was saying—the language wasn't English—but it was clear enough the two of them were arguing. At least, the woman was. The scowling man she was with had folded his arms across his chest, clearly annoyed at being hen-pecked. He snarled something back in a tone full of sarcasm, which served only to turn up the volume on his partner.

Seriously?

I glared at them, hoping the social pressure would make them take notice of everyone else on the train and dial it down. But neither of the middle-aged arguers even looked in my direction. Huffing a sigh, I glanced around. Were the other passengers as irritated as I was?

At the far front of the car, I caught sight of another man also watching the couple. Tall and muscular, with close-cropped hair that was nearly black and the scruff of a beard to match, he sat alone. Probably because of the force-field bubble of don't-mess-with-me-I-might-bite that extended at least five feet around him. I recognized the look from my brother. This was a man who could handle himself. Military, maybe. Or law enforcement. Definitely hot, either way. How had I missed seeing *him* when I boarded the train?

The male half of the fighting couple threw up his hands, uttering a spate of rapid-fire words that caused his seatmate to suck in a sharp breath through her nose.

That wasn't good.

The hottie at the other end of the train car slid his gaze to mine and shook his head a little. I offered a wry smile and an eye roll in return, and we shared a moment of empathetic annoyance over our circumstances, trapped as we were with these asshats. As our gazes held, I felt a frisson of something else. Definitely interest on my part, and as one corner of his mouth tipped up, I thought I saw a spark in his eyes as well.

Maybe that was wishful thinking. Either way, it was far more pleasant to contemplate than the problem awaiting me at home or these twats who were making a public scene.

As the couple had another outburst, my attention jerked back to them.

Right. There'd be no actual working in all of this.

Stuffing my laptop in my backpack, I stood and pulled my suitcase from the rack. I'd just find somewhere else to move. Maybe there'd be space in another car. Pushing my suitcase ahead, I edged into the aisle.

The hot guy caught my eye again and jerked his chin toward the empty row of seats across from him in clear invitation. It wasn't really far enough away to block out the sounds of this arguing, but I was too distracted to work anyway, so why the hell not?

Making my way down to his end of the train, I lifted my suitcase onto the empty rack above and dropped into the adjacent seat with a grateful smile. My companion nodded in silent acknowledgment of my thanks. Recognizing that this guy had been keeping to himself for a reason, I reached into my backpack and pulled out my e-reader. I could at least dip into the thriller I was working through in my spare time.

Except the gits behind me continued to make a racket.

I huffed another sigh. Why hadn't I remembered to pack my earbuds for this trip?

The stranger across from me leaned out into the aisle, raising his voice enough to call out to the couple. Whether it was the use of their language or the command in his deep voice that had even my lady parts sitting up to take notice, they shut up long enough to grab their things and leave the car, cheeks flushed bright with a mix of embarrassment and temper.

My shoulders relaxed as the noise in the train car dropped to a more comfortable level. "Thank you."

I had no idea where this man was from, or if he even spoke English, but I figured the gist would be clear enough.

"You're welcome."

When a familiar burr spilled out, I could only blink at him. "You're a Scot."

"So are you."

That was true enough. And it wasn't like it was unusual to run into a fellow Scot anywhere in the UK. Still, I hadn't been expecting that. "What language were they speaking?"

"German."

"Huh. What were they arguing about?"

"Evidently, he fouled up their booking and, instead of

flying, they're having to take the train and are missing a whole day of their vacation."

"Ah. So that was mostly an 'If I want something done right, I have to do it myself' sort of argument?"

"More or less."

I couldn't quite peg what region of Scotland he was from. Not the same part of the Highlands as me. Somewhere in the Borders maybe? Likely his accent was muddled a bit, as mine had been from four years of living in Edinburgh for university.

"What did you say to them?"

Those big, broad shoulders jerked in a shrug. "I reminded them that this was a public train and that no one wanted to listen to their yammering. Then suggested they ought to take their conversation elsewhere."

I grinned. "Well, thank you. That would've been a very unpleasant ride for the rest of us if they'd stayed."

He inclined his head and shifted to watch the scenery.

Message received. He didn't want to talk. That was fine. At least I could read in peace now.

Except as I tried to lose myself in the narrative, I could feel the stranger's eyes coming back to me. I glanced up, arching my brows when I caught him staring.

"Sorry. I just wondered what you were reading."

"*Loch of the Lost.*"

Humor lit his brown eyes, and he gave a sage nod. "There's been a murder." He deepened his burr to give extra roll to the R's.

"Are you a Lochlan Reid fan, then?" It was practically a requirement for anyone from our village, as Glenlaig was where Lochlan had settled a few years back, and we considered him one of our own.

"Aye. He's no' bad when I'm in the mood for tartan noir. Sometimes they're too dark for me, though."

I got that. I had to be in the mood for a body count. "What do you read instead?"

"Don't laugh."

I crossed my heart with one finger. "I wouldn't dare."

"Graphic novels."

"Like superheroes and such?"

"Sometimes. I like fantasy, too. And sci-fi."

"I prefer to watch my fantasy. Too many of the authors seem to feel they need to give two hundred pages of description of the setting and the magic and political system that doesn't actually move the plot. And there's never enough romance."

"A romance fan, are you?"

Because he didn't say it in a patronizing way, I didn't bristle. "Of course. What's the point of risking one's life to save the world if you don't get love in the end?"

Instead of rolling his eyes or dismissing my opinion as a lot of men would, his interest seemed to sharpen. "Fair point. That was the only real saving grace to Marvel's *End Game*. Steve finally got to be with Peggy."

Giving up all pretense of reading, I dropped the e-reader back into my bag. "Thank you! He was practically the only member of the entire MCU who got to be with the woman he loved. I don't know why male writers always seem to think the hero has to sacrifice everything and be alone in the end."

My companion hummed a noncommittal noise as something flashed over his face. "I imagine a lot of them would argue it's art imitating life. A lot of the things so-called heroes have to endure—male or female, for that matter—leave them so changed, it's not so easy to go back home."

Talk about art imitating life. If I hadn't been sure he was military before, I was now. But I didn't call him on it. If he wanted to speak of it, he would. For my part, I was content to keep our discussion on fiction. "There is nothing on earth more powerful than love. Nothing." I lifted my chin, daring him to contradict me.

His lips curved just a little. "Want to loan me some of that conviction?"

"I can give you a boatload of examples." And I did. Over the next couple of hours, we talked of books and films, debating how many popular ones could have been rewritten to have more hopeful endings. My companion was surprisingly well read, and I lost myself in the discussion, enjoying the low-key flirting I was pretty sure was happening.

He was older. Late twenties or maybe thirty. Old enough that he had actual life experience to back up his opinions. Not that he was sharing about those experiences. And that was fine. We were just two strangers on a train, enjoying some good conversation.

It wasn't until his gaze shifted from mine that I realized we were still sitting at one of the tiny stations we'd pulled into on the way. I'd been dimly aware of a couple of passengers getting off and more getting on. But that had been several minutes ago. We should've been on our way again by now.

My seatmate frowned. "Something's wrong."

As if he'd manifested it with his words, a tone sounded over the PA system, and the conductor asked for everyone's attention.

"Passengers, we have a problem."

3

ALEX

I went on high alert, my brain automatically running through scenarios where the train had been sabotaged. Who was the target? The person or group responsible? What was their motive? How quickly could we move all the civilians out of harm's way? Or was this a targeted attack? Kidnapping attempt?

"We've run into a little hiccup. Well, more than a little one. There's been a rockslide on the tracks north of here. Crews are already working to clear the mess, but it's going to mean a significant delay. Rest assured, we will work with all of you to assist in making arrangements for your connecting trains. In the meantime, feel free to step off the train to explore the village. You will receive a confirmatory text message when we're prepared to get underway again. If you do not have a mobile phone, please check back at the station in two hours."

Not sabotage. At least, probably not. I'd seen no evidence of an obvious high-value target when I'd boarded myself. So this was almost certainly a fluke. But the idea of staying on this unmoving train while they dealt with the issue made me want to climb the walls.

My seatmate reached for her backpack. "Well, I don't know about you, but I certainly can't imagine just sitting here for the next two hours. Want to get out of here?"

Was my paranoia that obvious?

But my charming companion showed no outward signs of being aware of my paranoia as she looked at me for an answer, brows arched.

I leapt at her offer like a lifeline. "Absolutely."

Gathering up our bags, we disembarked at the small station that nestled between two tracks. I'd been so focused on the conversation, I wasn't entirely certain where we were. This was the sort of small station that these lines frequently blew straight through. The sign on the building read Tarnside. A set of stairs led to a bridge that crossed from the platform, over the second set of tracks to the village beyond. The platform itself was crowded with other passengers who had the same idea.

I was still getting my bearings when I realized my seatmate had marched over to the ticket kiosk to speak with the woman behind the glass. I neared in time to hear her ask, "—within walking distance to grab a cuppa or a bite to eat?"

I was vaguely impressed that, while everyone else seemed at loose ends, she was already making a plan. Confident and capable. Both were attractive traits in a woman.

The ticket woman made some suggestion, and my new friend waved me toward the stairs.

"There's a wee cafe a couple of blocks away. C'mon."

Amused that she'd taken the lead, and content to let her, I fell into step and followed her up and over the bridge into Tarnside. The village itself looked to be maybe a couple of square miles laid out more or less in a grid pattern. The cobbled high street led straight down from the train station and was flanked by squat, whitewashed buildings that had been livened up with planters full of early spring flowers. At the end of the first block, she took a right and then a left onto the next street.

The Mossy Stone Cafe sat halfway down on the right. Its otherwise plain white exterior was interrupted by a deep green awning. A pair of garden gnomes flanked the door, and a gnome holding a cup of coffee, seated at a moss-covered stone table, was painted on the window glass. A handful of patrons filled tables inside. A couple of women who looked like young mums, and some old timers who lingered over their newspaper and a mid-morning cuppa.

I had already had breakfast, but I'd been up since the wee hours, so I could handle a bite to eat. I stepped up behind my seatmate at the counter.

The proprietress had a riot of gray-streaked curly hair pulled back into a knot. Her green eyes were lively as she flashed a smile. "Welcome to The Mossy Stone. What brings you to our little village?"

Why did she need to know that? Shouldn't she just be asking for our order?

Her gaze slid curiously between me and... how the hell had I not actually asked my seatmate's name yet?

The woman in question just smiled. "Oh, my professor and I were coming back from a conference in London when they had to stop the train."

Wait... what?

My seatmate continued, leaning forward in a conspiratorial fashion. "Apparently, there's been a rockslide on the tracks somewhere north of here. They say we'll be on our way in a couple of hours, but we were a bit famished, so here we are. A woman at the train station said you have the best pastries in town."

The proprietress beamed. "That we do."

"What do you recommend?"

Fascinated and more than a little curious why she'd spun this little tale, I kept my mouth shut other than ordering a tea and a sausage roll. Not until we settled in the far corner of the cafe with our food—my back to the corner and a clear sightline to the door—did I raise a brow in question.

She jiggled her tea bag and shrugged. "It's a small town. They want to hear something interesting, and you didn't want your personal business shared. This way the essentials got communicated, and she got to people watch."

Huh. That was not the explanation I'd expected. "Lots of experience with small towns?"

"I grew up in one."

"Is that where you learned how to shift the focus back on her so she stopped asking questions?" Because that had been masterfully done.

She twitched her shoulders again and sipped. "I'm good with people. Most like talking about themselves. Present company excluded."

"I don't dislike talking about myself." Hadn't we been talking for hours already?

She snorted a soft laugh. "Please. We've been talking all this time, and you haven't even mentioned your name. It didn't take much of a leap to assume you didn't want your personal business shared." There was no censure in her tone. Only easy acceptance.

I winced. "I'm out of practice just talking to people. I'm Alex."

Her smile came easy and full, lighting her eyes. "Ciara."

Damn, but those eyes were gorgeous. Tearing my gaze away before I fell into them and drowned, I sipped at my tea. "So… professor?"

Ciara nodded toward my jacket. "It's the tweed. It gives the vibe." Her full lips curved into a grin that popped a pair of shallow dimples in her cheeks. "You, however, do not."

She'd proved herself a perceptive woman, and I wondered what I'd given away when I was usually so locked down. "What vibe do I give?"

I thought she'd consider the question, but she instantly responded, "Military." When I only blinked, she continued. "I have family who served. I know the look."

I made a noncommittal grunt that was probably confirmation enough and bit into my sausage roll. But despite my own reticence, I wanted to know more about her. "Are you in university, then? Was that why you defaulted to the professor thing?"

"I'm in my last term. I'll be graduating at the end of the spring."

She'd be about twenty-two then. "From where?"

"Napier."

"So you're headed back to Edinburgh?"

"I am. You?"

"Going on to Inverness to visit a friend. Though, I'm not sure what the connection's going to look like with this delay. I was already going to be getting in late tonight." That was a problem for later in the day, when I had more information about the train schedule. For now, I was more curious about her. "Do you like it? Uni?"

I'd expected another easy answer, but this one seemed to make her hesitate. "I love the school. I love Edinburgh. But I'm still a little on the fence about what I'm studying."

"A bit late in the game to be deciding that, isn't it?"

Ciara grimaced. "Aye. That's the problem."

Was that what the worry was about? Or was there something else?

Before I could ask what it was she'd studied, she turned the tables on me. "What about you?"

When I didn't immediately answer, she held up a hand. "You don't have to say anything if you don't want."

But I found myself wanting to open up and give her... something. "I find myself in a bit of a transition. I'm trying to figure out what I want to do next with my life."

She lifted her mug of tea in a toast. "You and me both."

Feeling an odd sort of kinship, I tapped my mug to hers, grateful for the rockslide that was giving me extra time with her.

4

CIARA

The rumble of the train vibrated against my back, where I leaned against the window. "So you said you were trying to figure out what came next in your life. Do you only have to please yourself, or are you working around the expectations of family or a partner?"

As a means of finding out whether he was single or not, it wasn't exactly smooth, but I was aware of the dwindling distance to Edinburgh and the fact that our time together was drawing to a close. I needed to know because... well, reasons.

"I suppose family is always a consideration. I've a brother who's married. They live near our parents, so I've not had to worry overmuch as they've gotten older. They'd love to have me closer, but there's no pressure there, which I appreciate. And there's no partner to consider. In a way, I suppose that's harder. There's nothing to winnow down my options, which is a blessing and a curse. What about you?"

No partner. That shouldn't have made me want to do a fist pump, but knowing the way was clear for... anything had excitement fizzing in my blood.

"I'm lucky enough to have incredibly supportive parents.

And if I were to ask their opinions, they'd tell me to follow my heart. The problem being that I don't know what it's telling me other than the path I've been on isn't the right one." I blew out a long breath. "I haven't actually admitted that out loud before now."

Alex's lips curved in an understanding smile. "Sometimes that's easier to do with a stranger."

"True enough." Except he didn't feel like a stranger. All these hours of conversation had felt like running into an old friend and catching up. Which circled back to those reasons I'd been considering since our layover in Tarnside. I thought of that old 90s movie my mum loved so much and wondered if I dared make the ask for him to get off the train and spend more time with me. Because I dearly wanted this connection to go beyond just these hours on a train.

"Excuse me." A tired-looking man in a uniform stepped up to us. "I apologize for it taking so long for me to get to you. I've been working my way along the entire train. Where are you headed?"

"Getting off in Edinburgh," I told him.

"I'm going on to Inverness," Alex added.

The conductor consulted a tablet in his hands. "There is a connecting train to Inverness that you can pick up when we get to Edinburgh. We're about fifteen minutes out. It's a close connection, so you'll need to make a run for it once we pull into the station. But you aren't the only one going for that one, so they'll be delaying a bit."

"What's the arrival time in Inverness?"

The conductor checked the schedule and told him.

Alex nodded and pulled out his phone. "I'll let my ride know."

His ride. Because he had places to be, friends to see. His friend was likely already inconvenienced by the massive delay we'd had. I had no right to interrupt his plans any further. And if he actually wanted to talk to me past this train ride, he'd ask for my number. Right?

But he didn't ask for my number as the announcement was made that we were pulling into Edinburgh Waverley station. That was it, then. Putting on a bright smile to mask the stab of disappointment, I rose. "I really enjoyed talking with you."

His brown gaze came to mine. "Likewise. You made what would have been a very arduous journey a lot more fun."

Needing something to do so I didn't have to keep looking into those eyes, I reached up for my bag on the overhead rack. The train slowed to a final stop, and I lost my balance, tumbling straight into Alex's lap with a little yelp. His arms closed around me, and I lost my breath because holy hell, he was fit. I'd been looking at him all day, so I knew it objectively. But feeling the solid curve of his muscled biceps and the warm wall of his chest against me had my pulse pounding. No force on earth could have stopped me from looking at his mouth. My own went dry, and I swallowed. Damn, I wanted to kiss him. Wanted to know the feel of those perfectly shaped lips and how he tasted. Was I crazy enough to even try? Or had I been misreading signals all day?

"Ladies and gentlemen, welcome to Edinburgh Waverley Station. This is the final stop for this service. Please ensure you have all your personal belongings with you before you leave the train. Mind the gap between the train and the platform as you alight. If you are visiting Edinburgh, we wish you a pleasant stay. For those returning home, welcome back. If you have a connecting train, please see the departures board on the concourse. Thank you for traveling with us today. We hope you have a pleasant onward journey."

I slid off Alex's lap, and he didn't try to stop me.

That really was it, then. Regretting every inch of separation and all the lost opportunities, I retrieved my bag. "I've got to go. And so do you. You've got a connecting train to catch."

"So I do." He shoved to his feet and shouldered his bag.

Falling into the flow of other passengers, we made our way off the train and onto the platform. Because I traveled through here all the time and knew which line went to Inverness, I pointed. "Your platform is going to be that way."

He didn't move. One big hand curled around the strap of his bag, holding it on his shoulder. "It was really nice to meet you."

My heart kicked into high gear again. Was he going to ask for my number now? Should I take advantage of his hesitation and blurt out the invitation for him to stay a night in Edinburgh? Would I mean that how it sounded? Did I want him to stay the night not only with me, but *with* me?

Yes. God, so much yes.

Was that crazy? I barely knew this man. And yet...

And yet, he said nothing else, only stood there, seeming to wait for... something.

My shaky resolve crumbled. "You, too. Have a good trip to Inverness. And good luck with... everything." Flashing one more smile, I turned and walked away, cursing myself with every step.

Why couldn't I be braver and ask for what I wanted? Maybe he hadn't been interested in more than conversation, but I didn't know, now did I? Because I hadn't opened my mouth to make the offer. I'd thought about it. Imagined what I'd say. But in the end, I simply didn't have the follow through. But what else was new? I hadn't been brave enough to change the course of study I'd been questioning for a year. Why should I expect myself to have courage about anything else? Maybe all the courage in the family had gone to my brother. God knew, he'd made use of it for years during his military service.

Disappointed in myself, I checked my watch. It was well past when I'd been meant to meet my friends at the pub, but they never called it a night early. I'd drop my stuff off at my flat and drag myself out to meet them. A drink and a meal would surely help me shake off this sense of failure. At least for a little while.

Resolved, I merged into the crowd of people headed for the station exit.

5

ALEX

Rooted in place on the platform, I watched Ciara go, wishing with every fiber of my being that I'd kissed her.

She'd been interested. No question of that. She'd been looking at my mouth. The warm weight of her had felt so damned good in my arms, and I'd had to fight not to haul her closer and bury my nose in her hair. It had smelled of coconut and lime, like some sort of tropical drink. I'd taken a brief mental vacation to the South Pacific, imagining her tanned and toned, with sun streaks in her hair, wearing a teeny bikini and a sarong, drinking something tropical from a coconut with a paper umbrella, as she challenged me to... well... anything.

Then she'd been pulling away and saying she had to go. Reminding me I had a train to catch. I had to let her go. Didn't I? Ewan had already been forced to change his plans once to come get me. And Ciara needed to get back to her life. She didn't have room for a detour. That was all I could be. I didn't have a damned clue what came next in my life. I didn't have anything to offer someone like her.

The devil on my shoulder purred in my ear. *She doesn't know where she's going next, either. Who says you can't take a detour together?*

The idea of that was beyond appealing. Maybe it was because she was the first clear thing in this new phase of my life, and maybe it wasn't meant to last. But there'd been a genuine connection with her, damn it. More than simply physical attraction.

When was the last time I'd felt that?

Maybe never.

"Attention, please. The train to Inverness is now ready to depart from Platform 7. All aboard, please. Ensure you have your tickets ready for inspection. We remind passengers to mind the gap between the train and the platform as you board. This service will be calling at Haymarket, Stirling, Perth, Pitlochry, Aviemore, and finally, Inverness. We wish you a comfortable and pleasant journey. Thank you for choosing to travel with us today."

Dutifully, I turned in the direction Ciara had pointed, annoyed to find myself jostled by the herd of other passengers heading in the same direction. With every step, a vibration of wrongness pulsed through me, until finally I stopped.

I hadn't gotten this far in my life by ignoring my instincts. Why the hell was I walking away from her? I didn't have to do this. I could let Ewan know I wouldn't make it until tomorrow. Wasn't it worth the chance of following up with her, in case this wasn't just a connection of convenience? In case it was the start of something real?

I bolted back the way I'd come, dodging and weaving around other passengers as I desperately scanned the crowd for that dark head. There. Across the station at the coffee kiosk. I dashed toward her, only to pull up short as the woman turned, cup in hand, and I saw it wasn't Ciara. Turning again, I followed the crowd toward the exit. She'd been leaving. Another brunette with a rolling suitcase caught my eye near the doors. Closing the distance, I laid an arm on her shoulder.

The woman whirled with a little shriek, eyes going wide.

Not Ciara.

I immediately let her go, lifting my hands in a non-threatening gesture. "Sorry. I thought you were someone else."

When she backed away in a hurry, I wondered exactly how crazed I looked. Twice more I thought I caught sight of her. Twice more I was wrong.

"This is the final boarding call for service to Inverness."

As the announcement echoed through the station, I shoved a hand through my hair. This was my last chance to catch that train. If I sprinted, I could make it. Get to Inverness in time for Ewan to pick me up and drive me back to the village where he ran a pub now.

Or I could stay here and try to find Ciara.

With a population around half a million, Edinburgh wasn't a small city. The likelihood of just running into her again was slim. That would be like searching for a needle in a haystack.

But I was a man with a certain set of skills. I might as well use them for something other than work. Tracking down the woman who'd captured my imagination seemed like a more than worthy task.

Decided, I stopped to text my friend.

> Me: Not going to make it tonight. Will be in touch tomorrow with updated travel plans.

Man on a mission, I made my way out of the station. I had a woman to find.

6

CIARA

After arriving back at my flat, I almost didn't leave again. I was utterly demoralized that I'd let Alex walk away.

But what other option had there been? He'd had pre-existing plans, and our amazing day together hadn't obligated him to... anything. All undeniably true. Yet I couldn't shake the whisper of regret for the maybe of what could have been. Which I'd never know because I hadn't had the guts to ask for what I'd wanted.

Why hadn't I just taken a chance? If he'd said no, then I'd have had closure, and I wouldn't be any worse off than I was right now, save for a bruised ego.

Needing to escape my own crap mood, I changed into a favorite outfit and headed out to meet my friends at Thistle and Barrel. I'd texted earlier that I'd probably miss tonight because of the massive delay in my travel plans, but I didn't update them now. Better to give myself the out in case I got to the pub and realized I'd had enough peopling for the day and decided to nope out. At this point, it could go either way.

The pub was located a couple of blocks away from the more famous string of bars in Cowgate and was generally frequented by locals rather than tourists. I had always appreciated the neighborhood feel of the place. It reminded me of a more upscale version of The Stag's Head, the pub in the Highland village where I'd grown up. I stepped inside, feeling myself unwind at the sight of the familiar dark-paneled wainscoting and tartan wallpaper. As the warmth and din of conversation wrapped around me, I wove through tables, scanning the crowd for my friends. Though I spotted at least a dozen regulars, none of them were who I'd come to meet. Navigating to the bar, I waited until Elsie, the bartender on duty, came my way.

"Hey, Ciara. What'll it be tonight?"

"A pint of Thistly Cross."

"You've got it." Elsie moved to fill a pint glass.

"Did you notice where Ailish and Rory were sitting?"

"No, sorry. I haven't seen them tonight." She set the glass in front of me. "But we've been pretty slammed. I might've missed them. Do you want to start a tab?"

"No. Thanks." I paid for my drink and slowly wandered through the bar, hunting in the little nooks and corners where my friends preferred to nest for a night of drinking.

Finding no sign of them, I slid onto an empty stool and sent a text.

> Me: Where are you? I've been all through T and B's.

A few minutes later, a reply came back.

> Ailish: Oh my God, we didn't think you were coming, so we ended up at Dropkick Murphys.

I winced. The high energy atmosphere of the Irish tavern definitely wasn't my vibe tonight.

> Rory: Let us close out our tab here and come join you.

If they'd run a tab, chances were they were settled in right and proper. I hated to spoil their night, and now that I was out, I was back to regretting not opting to take advantage of the fact that my roommate was out of town for the weekend for some quiet. Then at least I could nurse my disappointment in private.

> Me: No, that's fine. I'm just going to finish my drink and probably call it an early night.

My friends tried for a few more minutes to convince me to join them, but I'd made up my mind. I wasn't fit company. Still, I took my time with the cider, knowing better than to simply guzzle it. Lunch had been hours before, and I definitely needed more than the snacks we'd had on the train. Should I order something here or hit up the chippy around the corner from my flat? Or maybe I could pop into the Tesco for some ice cream. They were all better options than taking my chances on what might be in the cupboards at home.

"Ciara! Fancy meeting you here."

The male voice pulled me out of my head. I glanced up and immediately wished I'd stayed home entirely.

After he'd pursued me for months, I'd gone out with Sean Thomson exactly once. That date had been more than enough to confirm what I'd already suspected—that he was far more interested in finding a woman to fawn over his perceived accomplishments and exploits than actually having a meaningful conversation. I'd politely declined going out with him again and had successfully avoided actually seeing him since. Looked like my two-month streak of luck was up.

"Sean." Why the hell hadn't I agreed to let the girls come meet me like they'd wanted? Then at least I'd have backup incoming.

He leaned comfortably on the bar beside me, invading my personal space bubble. "You haven't been answering my messages or calls." His lips were curved in a smile that told me he thought this was some sort of game.

"I didn't think we had anything further to say. We have nothing in common."

"That's part of the process! You needn't play so hard to get. I'm already more than interested."

Annoyed that he hadn't actually listened when I'd said I didn't care to see him again, I took a sip of my cider to buy time to think. Damn it, I hated hurting anyone's feelings, but it was more than obvious I'd have to be forceful with him. Guys like him simply didn't understand nice because their over-inflated egos didn't comprehend the fact that any woman wouldn't want what they had to offer. Of course, there was also the possibility that he wouldn't respond well to true rejection, in which case I'd simply draw on the self defense drilled into me by my former military big brother.

I really hoped it didn't come to that. It would cause a scene to drop him here in the middle of a crowded bar.

But as I opened my mouth to deliver a clarification Sean couldn't fail to understand, an arm slid around my shoulders and a familiar voice rumbled, "There you are."

Stunned and certain I hadn't heard right, I turned toward the new arrival. Alex's eyes were warm as he pulled me closer to his side.

"You're here." It was all I could think to say, even as I cuddled into him.

"Sorry I'm late." Something in his gaze shifted as his hand skimmed my cheek.

I wanted to ask what he was doing here, but I was too busy leaning into the warmth of his touch, like a flower seeking the sun.

Sean began to sputter. "Ciara, who is this... person?"

My personal miracle with the best possible timing.

Alex didn't spare him a glance. "Her boyfriend. Bugger off, mate." Then his fingers slid into my hair, and he lowered his mouth to mine.

7

ALEX

I hadn't actually meant to kiss Ciara. But I was so fucking relieved to have tracked her down, and I'd seen her facing off with this arrogant bam she clearly wanted nothing to do with. I just hadn't been able to help myself. Even then, I'd meant for it to just be light and easy. A casual claiming that the other bloke couldn't misunderstand.

But the moment my lips brushed hers, the attraction and tension that had been building between us all day detonated. Ciara's hands fisted in my jacket as she lifted to me, her mouth opening under mine. With a growl, I hauled her closer, needing to feel her against me, to reassure myself she really was here. That I'd found her. I wanted to drown in the sensation, in the tart, sweet taste of her against my tongue. It took all the strength I had to remember we were in public and pull away rather than allowing the kiss to spin completely out of control.

The blue of her eyes was almost completely swallowed by her pupils, and the heat in her gaze was nearly enough to have me diving in again. Instead, I made myself turn toward the other guy. Or, at least, where the other guy had been. Evidently, at some point, he'd walked away.

Right then. Mission accomplished.

But I couldn't seem to make myself let Ciara go. "Sorry about that."

Her brows drew together. "For kissing me?"

"Definitely not that." No reason to lie. "It's just... you had that handled without me coming in and... well, handling you. But I've spent the last hour and a half regretting not doing that on the train, and it seemed like the perfect opportunity."

Her lovely face relaxed. "Well, I'm not sorry, so can we both agree that wasn't a mistake?"

"Hell, yes."

She wasn't pulling away. Instead, her fingers curled into the belt loops on my jeans. "I can't believe you're here. How did you find me?"

As my cheeks heated, I was grateful the lighting in the pub wasn't exactly stellar. "Oh, well, I overheard your phone call when you got on the train this morning, saying you were meeting your friends at T and B's."

"Have you been here before?"

"No. I did a search of the restaurants and bars in the area. There were a couple of others that might have fit the bill, but I was banking on where you were going being somewhere closer to one of the universities, so I took a chance." If I'd been prepared to do more than that—well, I hadn't needed to resort to my other skills.

Ciara appeared suitably impressed. "Solid logic. So, why did you track me down? Just to satisfy your curiosity?"

What was it with everybody asking me questions I didn't know the answers to? But I'd give her what honesty I could.

"Look, I still have to be in Inverness tomorrow, but I couldn't resist coming to find you. Today was... unexpected, and I didn't want that to be the end of things." It was maybe more honesty than I'd given anybody in longer than I cared to remember.

"Neither did I."

Her voice was so soft I barely heard it, but those words were everything. Maybe not a promise, but a possibility we clearly both wanted to explore. So much of my life was up in the air that I wanted to grab onto this, to her, with both hands. Maybe that was crazy. But here I was.

Ciara swallowed. "So... you found me. Now what?"

"Well, I was hoping you'd be willing to hang out with me until I have to catch my train in the morning. I thought maybe you could show me your city."

Beaming a smile, she reached out and snagged her glass, draining the last of whatever she'd been drinking. "Let's go."

As she towed me toward the door, I hesitated. "Wait, weren't you here to meet someone?"

"They ended up going elsewhere because they thought I wasn't coming. I've got no other plans. Have you eaten?"

"Not since the snacks we had on the train."

"Me either. Come on."

As she led me out of the pub, I thought I'd happily follow this woman anywhere.

We ended up at a chippy several blocks away. The neon sign above the lintel read Calypso. When we strode inside, the man behind the counter looked up with a smile that flashed white in his medium brown face.

"Ciara, my love. Who have you brought me today?"

I couldn't quite peg the accent. North African, perhaps? Moroccan? There was a hint of French, muddied with plenty of time in the UK.

"We're in need of sustenance, Maury. I promised to introduce my friend here to the best fish and chips in the city."

Maury laid a hand over his heart. "And you bring him here to me. You honor me. Will it be the usual?"

"Absolutely. Two, please."

As Maury moved about behind the counter, sliding

generous portions of battered fish into oil, Ciara chatted easily with him, asking about his wife and how his children were faring in school. They laughed and joked with the ease of friends, and I found myself a bit envious. She wasn't from here, but she'd made connections. Done the thing I was so intimidated by. It was fascinating to watch.

Ten minutes later, we carried two piping hot bags of takeaway out the door, with Maury's cheerful goodnight ringing in our ears. When I started to peel back the paper, Ciara reached out to stay my hand. "You'll blister your fingers. I speak from the voice of experience. Give it a few minutes to cool. It'll be ready to eat when we get there."

"Get where?"

"You'll see."

She casually took my hand again, linking her fingers with mine as if she'd been doing it for years. Why should that small gesture make me feel so grounded and happy?

As we strode down the block, I caught sight of a wiry man with a beard, his eyes on Ciara. I automatically tensed as the guy approached, bracing myself to shield her, but when Ciara saw him, she beamed. "Hey, James! Aren't you missing someone this evening?"

"Och, I'm on my own. Richard took Bob to his knitting circle meeting tonight. I think they're making him jumpers."

Ciara laughed. "Do you think they'll be better than the gloves they tried at Christmas?"

"Aye, well, if Bob gets hold of the efforts and tries to 'eat' them, Richard willnae be the wiser, will he?" James said this with air quotes in a tone that suggested that the efforts of this knitting circle were less than perfect.

"You're a brave man, James. Tell Richard I said hello and give Bob a kiss for me, aye?"

"I will. Will you be by at your usual time next week?"

"Should be. See you then."

"We'll all look forward to it."

As the other man strode away, Ciara tugged me into motion again.

"What was that about?" And who the hell was Bob?

"That was James. He owns the laundromat I use. He and his partner, Richard, are the proud owners of Bob, who's the sweetest little English Cocker Spaniel rescue who ever did live. We have an arrangement. I'll toss in my laundry, and they'll keep an eye on it while I take Bob out for a walk to get my dog fix. It's a win-win for us all."

"It feels like you know everyone."

"Not everyone. But Edinburgh is really a big small town in a lot of ways. You have a routine, you see the same people. If you make an effort, people respond to that. I come from a small village originally, so it's normal for me to make conversation and get to know people."

I liked the idea of that. More, I liked the idea of being part of this community she'd built for herself. I was surprised by how much I wanted to latch onto her. Not just because of the attraction that had struck me like a mortar round, but because she quieted the vague sense of panic and paranoia. She made this transition feel possible. Which was maybe kind of crazy, but I hadn't felt this kind of connection with someone in... well... ever.

She cut through an alley and down another side street, making her way to a set of narrow stone steps that wound up between two buildings. They took enough turns that it challenged even my natural sense of direction.

"Are you dragging me off to your lair to have your wicked way with me?"

Ciara snickered. "You wish."

Aye, I absolutely do.

"We're almost there."

A dozen feet later, we emerged into a little walled courtyard garden. The space wasn't huge. Maybe twenty feet by twenty, hemmed in by old stone buildings on all sides. The clear night sky stretched out overhead, a blanket of stars. A quartet of stone benches were set at the compass points, surrounded by lush vegetation I wouldn't have expected somewhere in the city.

"Wow. This place is something. What is it?"

"I don't know. I got lost down here a couple of years ago and stumbled upon it. I've never seen another soul, not even someone to ask permission to be here. There's no other entrance but the gate there. But it's never been locked, so I keep coming when I need to get away and have some privacy in the city."

She dropped onto the northerly bench and patted the space beside her. "Come, sit. And tell me about your dreams."

Well, how could I turn down an invitation like that?

8

CIARA

Alex stared at me for so long, I wondered if I'd made some misstep. He seemed... not exactly flustered by the question—a man like him didn't seem to ever get flustered—but taken off-guard.

Not wanting to make him uncomfortable or do anything to destroy this fragile connection we were building, I started to backpedal. "You don't have to—"

"No." He shook his head, as if to clear it, and closed the distance to sink down on the bench beside me. "No, it's just been so long since I was free to dream that I hardly even know how to answer the question."

The idea of that broke my heart. Even if I didn't know exactly what I wanted to do with my life, I still had the capacity to dream.

Was this a product of his military service, or did it have something to do with his life or family circumstances? Somehow, I sensed if I tried to pry, it would shut things down between us, and that was the last thing I wanted. So, I kept my tone matter-of-fact. "Well, it seems like now is as good a time as any. You said you were at a crossroads. That suggests a choice.

What are your options? If you aren't limited by work or family, what would you want to do?"

Alex said nothing for a bit as he opened up his food and tasted. "Mm, this is really excellent."

"I'll be happy to pass that back to Maury."

The bench wasn't large, and there was little space between us. Even with my eyes closed, I would have been aware of him beside me. There was a gravity to him that pulled me. As I shifted, our knees brushed. A casual touch to test the waters, because I wanted to kiss him again. In truth, I wanted to do a hell of a lot more than kissing, but I'd take my time, see where things stood.

Leaning over, I nudged his shoulder with mine, reminding him he hadn't answered. "Do you have another job lined up? Interviews?"

"No. Not yet. I've only just left my old job."

Ah. It had taken my brother a while to figure things out, too, when he'd left the military. Not that Alex had confirmed that assessment.

Before I could prod again, he turned the tables on me. "What about you? You said you weren't sure about what you're studying. What is that?"

Fine. I'd give him this, if for no other reason than I was grateful for the possibility of finally talking about this with someone who wasn't involved.

"Well, I've spent the last four years in International Festival and Event Management. That's what I was actually doing in London. Working a big academic conference down there."

"You don't like it?"

"I loved it for a while. I studied abroad in the US for a semester, and I've met all sorts of wonderful people. I do truly love the planning and the organization, seeing a vision come together and go off without a hitch. I'm good at it, and the program I'm in has an outstanding job placement rate for graduates." These were all arguments I'd given myself many, many times to justify why I'd stayed.

When I didn't go on, he nudged my shoulder in return. "But?"

Somehow, it was easier to tell him the thing I hadn't been able to admit to anyone else.

"But I... There's just something that's not there for me. I don't like the scale. I'm not intimidated by it, but I come from a small village. I mean, you've seen me interact with people here. I like people. I like the intimacy of knowing them, and there's no real intimacy in this big festival planning stuff. It's this huge scale thing, and I just can't see myself doing that for the rest of my life."

"Sometimes it's hard, when you're really good at a thing, to consider leaving that thing and doing something else."

The statement rang with authenticity, and I wondered what it was he'd done in the military. But I didn't voice the question.

"True story." I folded my dinner wrappings into the bag. "Finished?"

"Aye."

"Want to keep walking?"

"Sure."

We gathered our trash and left the little hidden garden, winding our way back down to the street. Once we'd disposed of things in the bin, Alex took my hand in his. Those strong fingers felt incredible curled around mine, and I had to fight not to grin like a loon.

"So how could you apply those skills to something else that's not quite what you've been doing?"

Oh, we were still talking about this? I struggled to pull my attention away from the warmth of his hand. "What do you mean?"

"Think outside the box. Those skills of organizing events and so on and so forth are transferable. It's not just applicable to big festivals or large-scale whatever. Surely you could do that on a smaller scale with something else."

I'd been so focused on the problem, I hadn't considered the idea that I could make a lateral move to something else. Everyone around me had been doing the same thing I was. No one was talking about changing.

"Well, like you, I'll have to think about it. But I do feel better about the idea that it's not been an entire waste."

"Most skills are transferable to something else. Sometimes you just have to have a shift of perspective to see how. In your case, it's all logistics, aye? There's always a need for people who are good at logistics."

"True enough." Needing to touch him, I curled my free hand around the crook of his elbow, tipping my head to his shoulder. "Did you go to university?"

"Not traditionally, no."

"Have you ever thought about it? Completely changing what you're doing."

Alex stopped to look down at me and brushed the hair back from my cheek. "Well, I wasn't before, but the idea has a hell of a lot of appeal right now. You make the idea seem very appealing. Or maybe that's just you."

Now or never.

Heart in my throat, I rose to my toes and brushed my lips to his. With a low groan, he wrapped his arms around me, pulling me in. Nothing about this was for show. There was no one to run off. No one to perform for. This was just for us. And it was utterly delicious. *He* was utterly delicious, and I wanted him.

On a hum, I dropped back down, taking his hand. "Will you come with me?"

"Anywhere."

With that promise ringing in my ears, I led him another three blocks down to a scarred, black wooden door.

"Where are we?"

I swallowed.

"My place. Will you come up?" When he hesitated, I felt the need to clarify. "I know we only have tonight, but I feel a real connection with you, and I don't want to let that pass by."

If he begged off on some sort of noble grounds, I might just die of embarrassment.

But his heated gaze pinned me to the spot. "Neither do I. Are you sure?"

With a lopsided smile, I confessed, "I don't normally do this, but yeah. Yeah, I'm sure."

When was the last time someone had made me feel this seen?

Never. That alone was worth the risk.

His lips curved as he brought my hand up for a kiss that had my heart zooming like a hummingbird in my chest. "Lead the way."

I unlocked the door and led him upstairs to my third-floor flat. Somewhere between the street and unlocking my own door, my nerves kicked up. Alex followed me inside, looking around in a way that told me he was taking in every detail. I wondered what he saw. We were poor university students, so we didn't have that much stuff, and some of our furniture had been sidewalk or dumpster finds.

"My flatmate is out of town for the weekend, so we have the place to ourselves. It's not much, but it's my home away from home." God, I wished he'd kiss me again to kill these nerves so I'd stop babbling.

Taking his hand again, I began backing toward my bedroom, thinking to speed things along.

"Ciara." The low rumble of his voice had me stumbling, but Alex caught me, drawing me in until he took my mouth.

Oh, thank God.

I rose into him, opening for him, wanting, needing more. But he didn't speed up, didn't go deeper, instead taking his time to thoroughly make love to my mouth, until the nerves shifted into something else entirely. All the urgency to get to now, now, now simply melted into a loose, languorous sensation that drained away all rational thought but *More*. So I gave myself over to the kiss and happily resigned myself to let him lead.

9

ALEX

Recognizing Ciara's nerves, I set myself to the task of distracting her. Not that kissing her was any sort of hardship. I took my time about it, losing myself in the taste of her and the feel of her in my arms. My military service had taught me exactly how fragile and short life really was, and that pleasure and joy should be grabbed while they could. She was both, and I was holding on with everything I had. I didn't know if we'd have more than tonight, but I'd damned well make sure we both enjoyed it and had no regrets. That had been the whole reason I'd come after her.

Her long, lithe body went pliant against me, and that surrender fired my blood, challenging all my good intentions. Bringing up the mental map I'd made of her place the moment we'd stepped through the door, I began circling her toward the bedroom she'd been dragging me toward. At least, I hoped that was where I was headed. I didn't stop kissing her to find out.

We stumbled through a doorway, and my hand slid beneath her shirt to find skin. I'd been wondering all day what she'd feel like beneath my hands. Her muscles quivered as I traced that smooth, smooth skin. Wanting more, I began working at the buttons of her shirt, exposing more inches to explore with every flick of my fingers, until at last I could slide the fabric from her shoulders. It fell to the floor in a whisper, and I lifted my head.

She'd left on a single lamp. Its golden glow gilded her skin, highlighting her slim figure in jeans and a lacy pink bra that cupped her breasts. They were high and firm. A perfect handful, by my estimation.

As I drank in the sight of her, she lifted her chin with a half-smile. "See something you like?"

God, I loved that bravado.

"Absolutely." I traced a finger along the swell of one breast, just above the edge of her bra, and watched her nipples draw tight.

"Turnabout is fair play." She reached for me, dilated eyes focused on the placket of my shirt. Her fingers worked much quicker than mine had, and when she shoved the shirt off my shoulders, she gave a satisfied purr as she began to explore.

I closed my eyes, absorbing the feel of her hands running over my pecs, down my abs. My profession had necessitated keeping my body honed. If she wanted to enjoy the results of that, I wouldn't stop her.

But when her lips pressed high on my chest, above my left nipple, my heart stuttered. There were scars from my service, and she moved from one to the next, kissing each one with reverence and respect for the pain I'd endured. It was far more intimacy than I'd been prepared for, and it made me yearn. For what, I didn't quite know, only that she was at the center.

Hooking a finger beneath her chin, I took her mouth, swallowing the greedy sounds of pleasure she made as I reached around to release the clasp of her bra. I drew it down, letting it drop. Then her bare breasts were pressed to my chest, and my already hard cock went even harder, desperate to plunge into her. But I'd see to her pleasure first.

I tipped her backward, following her down to the bed and indulging myself by taking my mouth on a tour down her throat, across her delicate collarbone, and on to capture one rosy nipple in my mouth. She was so damned sweet and responsive, bowing up, her fingers diving into my hair with a grip that told me I absolutely shouldn't stop, even without the gasping litany of "Oh God, yes. Please. More."

Her hips moved restlessly, shifting beneath me until she'd worked one of my thighs between her legs, seeking the friction she needed.

I could do better than that.

Unfastening her jeans, I lowered the zipper and slipped one hand into her underwear to cup the warmth of her sex. She opened for me, and I slid one long finger into her drenched heat and curled.

"Alex!"

Damn if that wasn't the best thing I'd heard in years. She was so deliciously responsive. I continued to worship her breasts, following the rise and fall of her hips with my hand, sliding another finger into her tight channel and finding that sensitive nub with my thumb.

When she shattered around me, I thought that was a perfectly brilliant beginning. She was still limp as I tugged off her shoes and dragged down her jeans, leaving her bare. Her body was lovely and flushed with pleasure, those big blue eyes fixed on me.

"You okay?"

Her lips curved in a seductive smile. "I'm more than okay."

She looked like my every fantasy come to life, and I was pretty sure my zipper was leaving a permanent imprint on my cock. But still, not yet.

"I want to taste you."

Her eyes went impossibly darker, and she drew one knee up in invitation. I knelt, loving the feel of her heels against my back as I settled between her thighs. I blew gently on her sensitive flesh until she bucked and swore. With a chuckle, I took a firmer grip on her hips and lowered my mouth to her center.

There were those hands again, fisting in my hair. Harder this time. I loved the pleasure-pain of those tugs as I worked her, driving her up until she was gasping and writhing, begging for release.

She screamed my name again as she shot over the edge.

I didn't think I'd ever tire of that sound.

"So. Glad. You. Got. Off. The train," she gasped.

"Me, too." With a chuckle, I pressed another kiss to the inside of her thigh and eased back to retrieve a condom from my wallet.

Ciara watched as I toed off my boots and stepped free of my jeans. She kept watching as I rolled the condom on and gave my cock a stroke. "You're way over there," she murmured. But I didn't miss the way her throat worked as I settled over her.

I brushed another kiss to her collarbone. "You okay?"

She pressed both hands to my shoulders and pushed.

I immediately fell back. No way would I take this anywhere she wasn't willing to go.

But instead of scooting away, she followed, swinging a leg over my hips to straddle me. Bracing herself on my chest, she brushed my lips with a kiss and eased to notch me at her entrance. "You're not exactly a wee man, aye? This might take a little finesse."

"Take all the time you need."

Despite the two orgasms, her body was incredibly tight. Content to let her take complete control of the pace, I gripped her calves and fought to remain still.

Face a mask of fierce concentration, she rocked, taking me in inch by slow inch. Her breasts swayed with the motion, and I loved every second of the torture.

Pressing against my chest, she sat up, throwing her head

back with a moan of satisfaction as gravity did the last of the work, fully seating me inside her. "Oh, that's better. I'm so full."

She swiveled her hips, and I grabbed them to still her. "Now I need a minute."

God, she gripped me like a fist. I had to draw on all my considerable control to keep from popping off like an untried lad.

"Okay?" Her echo of my own question made me smile.

"Better than okay." I arched into her, and it was as if I'd fired a starter pistol. She began to move, slowly at first, then picking up speed. She rode me hard, and my blood quickened at her pace, demanding I claim and conquer.

Jack-knifing up, I reached for her, rolling until our positions were reversed. Her legs tightened around me, and I felt her nails drag along my back as I pounded into her to the rhythmic chant of her "Yes, yes, yes."

We whipped each other to a frenzy, mouths and bodies mating, until her body bowed beneath me, every muscle tightening around me, until I was dragged over the cliff behind her.

I had just enough presence of mind to roll us again before I collapsed on top of her. We lay in a heap of tangled, sweaty limbs, hearts thundering.

"Jesus God," I gasped.

She nuzzled my jaw. "Just Ciara is fine."

I laughed. I couldn't remember the last time I'd laughed after sex. Had I ever? Delighted with her, I nuzzled back. "You're a wee hellcat, aren't you?"

She stiffened and pulled back a bit. "Is that a bad thing?"

"Hell no. I loved it."

"Well, then."

Reluctantly, I crawled out of bed to take care of the condom. With the ease of long-time lovers instead of new ones, we cleaned up. Then Ciara climbed back into bed and patted the mattress next to her.

I'd never spent the night with a one-night stand before, but I didn't second guess it. I simply crawled in and tugged her close. She snuggled in as if she'd been made to fit just like this in my arms. We talked of little nothings, until she lapsed into sleep, her breath puffing warm and even against my chest.

I stayed awake for a long time after that, thinking about what came next, and what exactly I was willing to do to pursue this past tonight.

10

CIARA

I woke to the weak gray light of morning. A gentle rain pattered against the windowpane. It was the sort of day meant for sleeping in. Or staying in bed for other reasons. The heavy arm draped over my waist definitely had my brain tripping down that path, despite the fact that Alex and I had already turned to each other twice more in the night, wiping out the last of my meager supply of condoms.

No question, it had been the best sex of my life—not that there was a terrible lot to compare it to. But it wasn't just the physical. No matter how improbable, we'd connected. I liked him.

And he was supposed to leave today. The idea of that broke my heart.

I'd told myself that I'd be fine with just one night. He was the thing I'd been brave about, and it had paid off in multiple orgasms. My body ached in places I hadn't known it could ache, and I felt deliciously used in the best possible way. His morning wood brushed my backside, and I was already wondering if I could talk him into just one more round before he left. But I knew that just one more wouldn't be enough. I suspected just one more would never be enough. And anyway, I really needed to answer the call of nature and brush my teeth before anything else.

Holding my breath, I managed to extricate myself from Alex without waking him and crept to the bathroom. After doing my business and sending up a prayer of thanks to the inventor of toothpaste, I stared at myself in the mirror. My hair was an absolute mess. My cheeks were flushed, and there was a sparkle in my eye that definitely hadn't been there before. And I had beard burn in the most interesting places. No way could I ever forget last night. Nor did I want to. But I didn't want that to be it. I didn't want him to walk out of my life for good when he left my flat today.

Back in my bedroom, I automatically picked up the trail of clothes we'd shed. Living in such a small space, I'd become a bit of a neat freak. His wallet lay on the floor, where he'd dropped it. It flipped open as I picked it up, and I couldn't stop myself from checking his ID. Decent picture. Better than mine, for damned sure. My gaze skimmed his name. Alex Conroy.

"What are you doing?"

I didn't jolt at the rasp from my bed. I dropped the clothes and wallet onto the chair in the corner. "Well, I was hoping you had a spare stashed in your wallet since we went through the rest of mine last night. But it appears we're out of luck."

"More's the pity." Alex stretched with a delicious growly morning groan that was sexy as hell. So was the way the sheet pulled low on his belly.

Putting on a flirty smile, I jerked a thumb toward the bathroom. "I was about to grab a shower. The hot water doesn't hold out particularly well, so if you want one yourself, you'd probably best join me."

His lips curved, and his eyes sparked as he dragged off the covers and stalked toward me, fully naked, his erection saying he was already completely on board. "Well, now. That just sounds sensible."

Those hands were on my bare skin again, and my knees went weak, my body already softening for his. "We'll have to get creative to take care of this." I wrapped a hand around his length.

Alex backed me into the bathroom, dipping to nibble at my throat. "I feel certain we'll figure it out." And we did. At least until the hot water ran out, and he manfully shielded me from the icy spray without even yelping. Well done him.

Afterward, we dressed, and I searched the cupboards to scrounge up some breakfast, or at least the makings for tea or coffee. There was next to nothing. Even the fridge was all but bare. "It's slim pickings, I'm afraid. I've been gone for weeks, and obviously my flatmate hasn't been to the market. Do you want to go grab something? I know a great little breakfast place not far from here."

Alex stroked the hair back from my face. "There's nothing I'd like more. But I have to go. I do still have plans with my mate up in Inverness."

"Oh, right." I tried to squash the disappointment. I'd known this was coming, and I'd tried to put it off in hopes he'd change his mind and his plans yet again.

"But I want to see you again. Can I have your number?"

Excitement exploded in my chest. "I thought you'd never ask."

We swapped contact information, and each sent a test text to make sure we hadn't entered the numbers wrong. Then Alex pulled me into his arms and laid his lips over mine in a long, lingering kiss that left my head spinning. He tasted of yearning and promises and everything I hadn't let myself want.

At last, he pulled back. "I'm not going to say goodbye. I'm just going to say, 'See you later.' Because I will. As soon as I know what my plans are, you'll be the first to know."

I wanted to leap around my flat like the Energizer Bunny on speed. But I held in my excitement. "I like the sound of that. I'll walk you down."

"No. I want to remember you right here, like this." He lifted my hand to his lips. "See you soon, Ciara."

Then he was gone. The door to the flat closed with a quiet click.

I stayed where I was for a minute, listening to the sound of his footfalls going down the stairs. When I could no longer make them out, I loosed a long, contented sigh and fell back onto the sofa, kicking and flailing my arms with a squee.

Things between us weren't over. They were only just beginning, and I couldn't wait.

11

ALEX

I shut the passenger side door of the SUV. "Thanks for picking me up."

Ewan McBride glanced over from the driver's seat. "It's no problem. I didnae expect the delay to take too long. Must have been one hell of a rockslide."

I shifted in my seat and rubbed at the heat on the back of my neck. "Aye, well, I could actually have made it here last night, but—well—I met someone."

My former section leader arched a brow and cranked the engine. "Having a little celebration for being done with your service?"

Temper kindled. "It wasn't like that. She wasn't just some quick lay." I thought of her smile and all the hours of easy conversation. "I think there's really something there. It's making me seriously consider Edinburgh as my next step."

"For her?"

"For her, and maybe for school. I'm thinking about working on an advanced degree. Maybe getting some more credentials to back up the skills I already have from the Royal Marines."

"That's certainly an option."

Nothing in Ewan's tone indicated approval or disapproval, but I couldn't help but wonder if that careful neutrality was an indictment in and of itself. Or maybe that was more of my paranoia talking. How long would it take me to shed that in civilian life?

"Have you heard from Patterson or Quinn?" The question dragged me out of my head.

"Not since they left on their latest mission." The last two members of our quartet were still serving. "We had drinks a couple of weeks ago, though."

"How were they?"

I considered the question. "Quinn is... Quinn. Driven. Still running from the devil on his shoulder. Patterson... I think now that you and I are gone, he'll start thinking about getting out."

Ewan grunted a noncommittal noise, but I knew that grunt.

"You're worried about Quinn."

"Been worried about him for years. That's nothing new."

"You and I both know it'll take death or a career-ending injury to make him walk away."

"That's what I'm afraid of."

We spent the rest of the drive to the village of Glenlaig catching up. Located in one of the more remote parts of the Highlands, I understood the appeal. If not for the unexpected gift of Ciara, I'd have likely considered settling some place like this. Being near my friend. Doing... well, I had no idea what. That hadn't changed since yesterday. But there was Ciara, and I wasn't fool enough to ignore adding her into the equation.

Ewan turned onto the high street of Glenlaig, driving past the quaint shops with brave pansies adding a pop of color from boxes out front. When he bypassed The Stag's Head Pub—which he owned and ran these days—I took a more careful look around.

"Where are we going?"

"To my parents' house. Mum is insistent on feeding you dinner."

"I remember your mum's cooking. It's pure dead brilliant. I'm certainly not going to turn down a home-cooked meal."

Fifteen minutes later, we pulled up in front of a single-story white bungalow that wasn't dissimilar to where I'd grown up. We trooped in the back door, careful to wipe our boots before tracking mud in on the scarred wooden floors.

"Mum! We're here!" Ewan bellowed.

A few moments later, a short, soft woman with gray streaked brown hair bustled into the kitchen. She made a beeline for me. "You're here! Oh, Alex, it's so good to see you."

I folded her in, enjoying the warmth of her maternal embrace. "And you, too, Mrs. McBride."

"Now, how many times must I tell you to call me Bonnie? You know I consider you one of mine."

"Thanks for that. I appreciate you having me for dinner." The scents of roasting meat and vegetables filled the room, making my mouth water.

"I couldn't have you come to town and not feed you."

"Cardinal sin, that," Ewan muttered.

"Oh, wheesht."

"Where's Da?"

"Here. Just finishing up out in the garden." Ewan's father, James, tugged off a glove and offered his hand. "Good to see you again, lad."

I shook it. "And you, sir."

"Dinner will be ready shortly. James, finish up whatever you're doing. Alex, please head into the lounge and make yourself comfortable."

"She disnae like having anyone underfoot in her kitchen," James advised.

"Because you're all thieves, dipping into things before I'm ready to serve."

James winked. "It's your own fault for being such a good cook."

Bonnie snapped a dishtowel. "Go on with you." But she was grinning as she said it.

"Son, I'm glad you're here. I need a second pair of hands."

"Sure, Da."

I started to follow them out. "I can help, too."

"No, no. It's just a wee thing. Sit and relax."

I wasn't that great at sitting and relaxing. Particularly not in new places, even if I did know the people. So, as Ewan and his father went out back, I began to prowl the lounge. It was a comfortable space, with a well-worn sofa and battered furniture that was loaded with character and told the story of a life well lived. There were photos of that life everywhere, and I spotted shots of a younger Ewan with arms around a red-headed lass and a blond lad who both looked a bit younger than him. There were photos of him as a wee lad that were proof he hadn't always been the serious man he was today. Another picture showed him around ten, holding a baby wrapped in a pink blanket. Ah, that was right. I dimly remembered he had a much younger sister who'd been a happy accident.

I moved on to the next wall, where the gallery continued, and stopped dead. A familiar smile shone out of the frame. My brain stuttered and stalled out, unable to make sense of what was in front of me.

Ewan strode up. "Oh, that's my baby sister, Ciara. She's off at uni."

His words seemed to come from far away, but their meaning drilled into my brain, nonetheless. In dawning horror, I had to acknowledge the truth: I'd spent all night worshipping my best friend's little sister.

Oh fuck.

What the hell was I going to do now?

∼

OH, Alex is in trouble now! Life is about to get Complicated in a Big Way. Stay tuned for the rest of Alex and Ciara's story in *Before Highland Sunset*, Book 1 of the Special Ops Scots series, releasing in October!

> I should never have touched her. I didn't know she's my **best friend's little sister**. When I found out... well... My life went off the rails, and we didn't see each other again.
>
> Now three years later, we're in the same **small town**, and she hates my guts. But when her ex won't take no for an answer, it's me she improbably reaches out to for help.
>
> Sure we can **fake a relationship** to keep him off her back. We've done it before. Except there's nothing fake about the heat between us. Or the very real threat from my past that's the true reason I ghosted her. Maybe she'll finally give me the chance to explain.
>
> I'll do anything to protect her, even facing down her brother for a **second chance**.
>
> One click to preorder Before Highland Sunset, a woman in trouble, protector in a kilt, brother's best friend small town romance today!

MEANWHILE, check out the Kilted Hearts series about Ciara's home village of Glenlaig, which begins with *Cowboy in a Kilt*. Keep reading for a sneak peek! Or jump ahead to *Protector in a Kilt* to get to know Ciara's big brother Ewan.

SNEAK PEEK COWBOY IN A KILT

A cowboy without a home

Screwed out of the family ranch that was his rightful inheritance, Raleigh Beaumont is a man with no roots and no purpose. When a friend drags him to the bright lights of Vegas, he figures he's got nothing to lose. But after a hell of a lot of whiskey and a high stakes poker game with a beautiful stranger, Fate hands him a second chance: An estate in the Highlands of Scotland. It's far from everything he's ever known, but he's willing to trade his Wranglers for a kilt.

An heiress with a crumbling heritage

When her brother's bride goes AWOL just days before the wedding that's meant to save their ancestral home from the mad marriage pact that's held their family captive for generations, Kyla McKean believes they've been granted a reprieve. Until she finds out about the new, single—male—owner of Lochmara and knows she's next in the hot seat or ownership of both their estates revert to the crown.

A modern answer to a three-hundred-year-old problem.

Kyla's desperate to save Ardinmuir. She proposes a marriage of convenience. One year as husband and wife to satisfy the pact, then they get a quick and quiet divorce. Raleigh's already lost one legacy. He'll do anything to keep from losing another, even tie the knot with a stubborn stranger who feels far more like ally than adversary.

∼

"It always rains the day a good man dies."

Raleigh Beaumont felt a smile tug the corner of his mouth, because the weather was bone dry. They'd been in a drought for the past few weeks. "Mama used to say that. She'd also say not to speak ill of the dead."

"Your daddy was probably the only thing your mama and I really disagreed on." Charlotte Vasquez came to lean beside him on the split-rail fence bordering the north pasture, propping one booted foot up as they both looked out over the rolling hills of the East Texas ranch that had been in his family for generations. "Luther Beaumont was a bastard, and we both know it."

"You're not wrong." One corner of his mouth quirking, Raleigh glanced down at the tiny Latina woman, who barely came to the top of his shoulder.

When Raleigh's mama, Lily, had been diagnosed with stage-four cancer, it had been Charlotte who'd taken a leave of absence from her job as a high-powered executive and moved in to care for her—and by extension, Raleigh. His daddy hadn't stuck around to watch Lily's decline as illness stole her vitality and vivaciousness, leaving her only a shell of the woman she'd once been. Luther had thrown himself into keeping the ranch running smoothly. At the time, Raleigh had convinced himself his father was only outrunning the inevitable grief. That he was protecting the legacy he'd married into.

He'd learned better since.

"I mean, come on," Charlotte continued. "He moves that

little hussy—" Said hussy being Twila, Luther's second wife, who was a bare seven years older than Raleigh himself. "—into the house when your mama's barely been six months in the ground? She only married him for his money, and he married her for the trophy." Her tone rang with bitter judgment, though it had been nearly fifteen years.

Raleigh stretched an arm across her shoulders, tugging her in for a hug. In the wake of Lily's death, Charlotte had convinced Luther to let her stay on as housekeeper, so she'd be around as a mother-figure to Raleigh because, God knew, Twila didn't have a maternal bone in her body. Back then, he hadn't understood what she'd given up for him, but at sixteen, that link to the mother he hadn't wanted to forget had saved Raleigh. And though he was well grown now, somehow, Charlotte had never left. He'd once asked her why, and she'd told him that losing his mother like that had shown her there were far more important things in life than breaking her back to climb a corporate ladder, and until she found another of them, she was staying planted near him.

"You didn't have to be here today. I'm a big boy. I can handle the reading of the will."

She squeezed him back, her head only coming to his shoulder. "Of course, I did. You need somebody here who's an ally."

They both turned to see a black Ford F-150 pulling up in the circular drive in front of the house.

"Looks like you weren't the only one with that idea," Raleigh murmured.

A familiar lanky figure climbed out of the truck and headed in their direction. Ezekiel Shaw was one of Raleigh's oldest and best friends. The one who'd as often been the instigator of mischief as the one to help him out of it.

Charlotte shot him a knowing smile. "Hey, Trouble."

Zeke grinned and pulled her in for a hug of his own. "Hey,

Charlotte. When you gonna run away from this place and marry me?"

"I can't marry you. Who'd be around to keep this one on the straight and narrow once he takes over the ranch?"

He clutched his chest in dramatic fashion. "Breakin' my heart, woman."

"Somehow, I think you'll survive." But a twinkle in her rich chocolate eyes softened the dry retort.

Turning to Raleigh, Zeke hauled him in for a back-thumping hug. "You holding up?"

"Ready to get this show on the road. What're you doing out here?"

Zeke pulled a flask out of his pocket and offered it. "Figured I'd be around for moral support, just in case."

Raleigh waved away what he knew would be bourbon. "You think things won't go well with the reading of the will?"

He shrugged. "Got no reason to think one way or the other. I just know you and Twila don't exactly get on."

"She'll be out of my life soon enough." And thank God for it. Raleigh was itching to truly take over the reins and begin implementing the plans for diversification and modernization that his father had rejected.

"From your mouth to God's ear," Charlotte muttered.

A whistle sounded behind them.

Hamp Browning, the family attorney, waved from the front porch. "Come on! It's time."

They strode toward the house, where Zeke dropped into one of the rocking chairs on the porch. "We'll see you on the other side."

Charlotte squeezed his shoulder once. "We'll be right out here."

Raleigh followed Hamp back to Luther's study. Kitted out in lots of wood and leather, the room still smelled of his daddy and the cigar he habitually allowed himself at the end of the day. He could just imagine the old man leaned back in the chair behind the massive desk set in front of the picture window that framed their spread. But it wasn't his seat anymore. After today, it would be Raleigh's.

Twila sat in one of the two chairs in front of the desk, looking like she'd come dressed for a board meeting instead of the reading of a will at home. She'd never fit in around here, with her city airs and high-heeled shoes. He didn't think he'd ever even seen her on a horse, and the only time she'd come out to the barn was to track down her husband. God forbid she risk stepping in something in her Feragucci shoes. Raleigh figured she'd be lighting out of here almost as soon as the reading was over. Back to Dallas, to her high-society friends.

He lowered himself into the other chair as Hamp circled around to the opposite side of the desk. The old man sat with a creak of springs and leather, running a hand down the tie that fell to the paunch overhanging his belt, then back up to smooth his big walrus mustache. Not for the first time, Raleigh thought he wouldn't look out of place as an extra in a western. Maybe in a leather vest at a poker table or behind the bar in an old saloon. The thought of it had his lips twitching into a smile. His mama would've appreciated the image. She had loved her westerns.

On a sigh, Hamp opened the folder he'd placed on the blotter. "Let's get to it, shall we?"

As the lawyer fell into the drone of legalese, reading the last will and testament of Luther Alexander Beaumont, Raleigh's gaze strayed past him to the window. Just a little while longer, then he'd finally be free to speak to the hands and their families, giving them the reassurance that nothing would change. They wouldn't lose their homes or jobs. His mind shifted to what needed to be his first orders of action. He'd had plenty of time to consider that, but he had to think about the season and what expenses the ranch would have coming up.

Abruptly, Raleigh realized Hamp and Twila were staring at him.

"I'm sorry. I zoned out there for a minute. Can you break it down into layman's terms?"

Hamp glanced at Twila, then back at him, his expression apologetic.

What the hell had he missed? Fighting not to curl his hands around the arms of the chair as a bad feeling set up like Quikrete in his gut, he waved at Hamp. "Go ahead; spit it out. I don't care about the money. I just want the ranch."

The old man winced. "Your father left everything to Twila."

That couldn't be right.

Shock was the only thing that kept his voice level. "I'm sorry. What?"

"All of it. He changed his will a few years ago. The stock, the land, the house. It all belongs to her now."

Raleigh exploded up, sending his chair skidding several feet back as he rounded on his father's wife. "This is fucking bullshit. This is my birthright. My mother's family's land. You have no right to it whatsoever. You don't want this place. You have no interest in running a ranch."

Unperturbed, she lifted her chin, somehow managing to look down her nose at him from where she stayed seated, her long legs crossed neatly in the slim pencil skirt. "You're right. I don't. Which is why I've already made arrangements to sell it."

The blood drained out of Raleigh's head. "Sell it? To who?"

She named a developer who'd been sniffing around for years with designs on turning their several thousand acres into cookie-cutter suburban houses.

As he let loose a string of profanity and began to pace, Twila examined her manicured nails. "You're welcome to try to beat the price." The figure she quoted was stratospheres above what Raleigh could afford.

When he said nothing, she flashed a smug little smile.

"That's what I thought." She turned back to Hamp. "If that's all?"

At his short nod, she picked up her designer purse. "You have a week to clear out." Then she strode out of the room without a backward glance.

Raleigh scrubbed a hand over his head. "This can't be happening."

Hamp shoved up from the chair, looking about ten years older than he had when he'd sat down. "I'm sorry, son. There's nothing we can do."

"Can I take her to court? Contest the will?"

"You can try. But in my professional opinion, it's going to cost you more than you've got, and you're not going to come away with a ranch in the end. Luther was in his right mind when he changed his will. The bastard screwed you right and proper. There's no two ways about it."

The sucker punch of it had Raleigh swaying on his feet in a way the loss of his father had not. It threw him back to the devastation of his mother's death. He'd promised her he'd take care of the ranch. Take care of the people who worked there. Carry on their family legacy. And all of it had just been ripped away.

He didn't even remember leaving the room, not until he almost ran over Charlotte.

"Honey, what happened?"

Raleigh just shook his head and kept going. He needed out of the house, into the hot, humid air.

As soon as he hit the front porch, Zeke pushed up from the rocking chair he'd commandeered. "What the hell happened?"

"I got fucked, that's what happened. The old man left her everything. All of it. The entire ranch. My *mother's ranch*. She's selling it to fucking developers. It's gonna be a goddamn neighborhood here next year. My home is liable to be bulldozed or turned into some kind of clubhouse. Not to mention what the hell happens to all the hands and their families." Heart sinking, he scrubbed both hands over his face. "I promised them I'd look out for them, and there's not a damned thing I can do about it. She gave me a fucking week to get out."

His gaze caught on Charlotte's face. Her expression had turned carefully neutral, but she'd lost all color. He realized he wasn't the only one out of a home.

"Fuuuuuck." Zeke drew the word out. "Man, I'm sorry. I don't even know what to tell you. I mean, I could—"

Raleigh held up a hand, knowing what he was about to suggest. "Not an option. Thank you, but no."

"Alright. Well, in that case, I'm thinking the best option is gonna be for you to get the hell out of town before you do something you're gonna regret."

Raleigh had no idea what he might do if he stayed and wasn't much inclined to risk ending up behind bars. And yet. "I can't just leave. I need to break the news to the hands. Do what I can to help them find other placements. And I should pull together the family momentos before that bitch tosses them all." The idea of losing anything else of his family history made Raleigh sick.

"I've already done a lot of that, setting things aside for you over the years," Charlotte assured him. "It won't take long to pull together the rest. We should probably hurry before that harpy gets it in her head you don't have a right to them."

Zeke pulled out his phone. "I'll make the arrangements for boxes and storage."

As his friend stepped away, Raleigh took Charlotte by the shoulders. "I don't know where I'm gonna land with all this, but wherever it is, you'll have a place there. Always. You're family."

She cupped his cheek. "You're a good boy, Raleigh, and you grew into a fine man. Your mama would be proud. Now, let's go get to work."

∽

"Maybe no one will notice."

Kyla MacKean briefly shot her brother some side eye. "Aye. Right. No one will notice the six-foot-wide chunk of plaster that's crumbled off the wall." The remains of that plaster lay in a heap on the scarred hardwood floors she'd only just waxed and polished for the wedding reception set to be held here in a matter of days.

Connor shrugged with his usual insouciance. "It's a six-hundred-year-old castle. We'll say it's part of the ambiance."

"Be serious, Con. This is important. We can't afford for anything else to go wrong. Too much is riding on this weekend."

The reality of living in a centuries-old castle in the Highlands of Scotland was nowhere near as romantic as books and movies made it out to be. It was cold, drafty, and often wet. Parts of the castle were fully uninhabitable. The estimates they'd received from various contractors for truly weatherproofing the place were astronomical. Every single problem they discovered was usually a sign of a bigger, deeper issue that called for bigger, deeper pockets than they had. The truth was, they were land rich and house poor, and without a massive influx of cash, the home they both loved would fall to ruin. And while Scots did love their ruins, Kyla wasn't keen on living in one.

She had a plan. One that involved using her brother's wedding as an opportunity to show the world that Ardinmuir could be a premier wedding destination. People paid big money for that sort of thing. But not if the bloody walls of the great hall were falling down around their ears.

"Dinna fash yourself. It's stood for this long. It's no' gonna crash onto our heads this weekend."

"So say you."

He swung an arm around her shoulders and squeezed. "Aye, I do."

"Oh good. You've got your line down." She teased him out of long habit, but in truth, she was worried.

"That's right. Until I do my bit as the sacrificial groom, your bit hardly matters."

Kyla spun into him, clutching his shirt. "You're not thinking of backing out, are you?"

His beleaguered sigh didn't make her feel any better.

"No. I know my duty. I've had a lifetime to accept it. This wedding will happen, and the terms of the marriage pact will finally be satisfied."

Then the axe hovering over all their heads because of an agreement made by ancestors who'd long since turned to dust would be gone, and they could get down to the serious business of actually saving the estate.

"I hope you know how much it means to me that you're doing this. I know Afton isn't who you'd have chosen."

"I'm certain I'm not her first choice, either. But it is what it is. We're friends. That's a far better basis than many have in arranged marriages."

Afton Lennox was the remaining heir to the barony of Lochmara, the neighboring estate. Her legacy fell under the same threat as their own, and Kyla could only thank God that she was willing to adhere to the terms of the pact. Then again, if she didn't, both their estates were forfeit to the Crown. Kyla would never stop cursing their ancestors for the addition of that little failsafe to the agreement meant to ensure the alliance between their families actually happened.

Knowing there was no changing their situation, she shook off the frustration. "We need to get someone out to look at it to make sure it's not going to get worse before the wedding. I don't want to have this place full of guests only to have plaster crashing down onto plates at the reception." Already feeling the beginnings of a headache, Kyla headed for the door. There was no getting mobile reception inside three- to four-foot-thick stone walls. "Maybe we can have a quick patch job done to get us through, then deal with the more permanent repair after."

It wasn't ideal, but she simply didn't have the bandwidth to deal with more disasters right now.

Connor followed her out. "I'm gonna go check in on Uncle Angus. The latest iteration of the wedding cake should be about ready."

"But the cake was decided on weeks ago! Why is he mucking around with it?"

"He reckons it'll be good practice for his audition for the *Great British Baking Show*, and who am I to turn down more cake?"

Kyla closed her eyes and prayed for patience. She loved her great uncle and her brother, both, but sometimes dealing with them felt like wrangling a couple of cheerful puppies rather than grown adults. At least if Angus was baking, he wasn't out getting into some other sort of trouble. And, really, she wasn't going to turn down more cake, either, given how the day was shaping up.

It took longer than she wanted to get ahold of Theo Gordon, the contractor who'd done the most work on Ardinmuir. And longer still to convince him to come out today, after he finished up the job he was working the next village over. If a batch of Angus's jaffa cakes had been promised as a bribe, well, she'd run into Glenlaig to pick up ingredients herself, if she had to. It wasn't like they could finish setup until this was sorted, anyway.

Satisfied that she'd done all that could be done for the moment, Kyla made her way down to the kitchen, which was housed in the newer portion of the castle. New being relative, having been added on in the nineteenth century, when James MacKean, head of the family at the time, had been flush with cash from a shipping empire that later collapsed. But at least that part of the house had been comparatively modernized.

As she stepped into the kitchen, Angus straightened at the heavy wooden island, lifting his piping bag in triumph from a truly lovely confection of swirls and flowers.

Kyla sniffed the air and caught the tang of citrus. "If that's a lemon chiffon cake, I just might fall to my knees and weep with gratitude."

Angus's blue eyes twinkled. "Then ready your tissues, lass. But you'll have to wait until I take a picture for my blog."

"We have a deal. Although you may take that back when I tell you that the only way I could get Theo out today to look at the wall in the great hall was to promise him a batch of your jaffa cakes."

One white brow winged up. "And what'll you trade *me* in this bargain?"

"My undying gratitude." Kyla slid her arm around him, and pressed a smacking kiss to his leathery cheek, feeling a bit of a pang as she realized he'd gotten a little more frail over the winter. Other than Connor, Uncle Angus was the last of her immediate family. When had he last gotten a checkup? She added that to the never-ending list in the back of her brain. Something to address after the wedding.

Connor snagged an Irn Bru from the avocado green refrigerator and kicked back against one of the long stone counters, smirking. "That disnae sound like much of a deal to me."

She pointed a finger at him in warning. "You stay out of this."

Angus considered. "You do the second round of dishes, and we have an agreement."

"Done."

As they shook on it, someone knocked on the door.

Connor pulled it open. "Malcolm! Welcome. Did you come

to help with the setup for the reception, or did you hear a rumor that there's more cake?"

The brawny, fifty-something man stepped into the kitchen, kilt swinging, his thick-soled boots thumping on the hardwood floors. His hazel gaze slid over the cake on the island, but his expression didn't change. There were some in Glenlaig who believed Lochmara's estate manager to be surly, but Kyla knew the truth. He just preferred animals to people. In social settings, he tended to be a man of few words. Still, the prospect of cake usually would have garnered at least some interest.

A frisson of unease traveled down her spine as she registered the tension in his burly shoulders and jaw. "Is everything all right, Malcolm?"

"No." His throat worked. "Afton is gone."

The words hit Kyla like a well-aimed stone to the gut. "Gone? What do you mean she's gone? The wedding is in less than a week. She can't be gone."

"I found a note."

"Saying what?" Connor asked.

"That she's sorry."

"That's it?" Kyla knew her voice was edging into the realm of shrill, but couldn't seem to control it.

"That's it."

Like a puppet with cut strings, she dropped into a nearby chair. "You can't be telling me what I think you're telling me. If she's gone... If she doesn't go through with this wedding, we're all screwed. The Crown has been watching since we filed the paperwork for the marriage. We have to find her."

"Her car is still in the village. I tracked her that far before I came here. But she's gone. She could be anywhere."

"What about the police?" Angus asked.

"Since she left a note, we have no reason to get them involved. She's not a missing person since she left voluntarily."

Malcolm spread his hands. "Unless you want to pour money into a private investigator to track her down…"

That was money they didn't have.

This was terrible. Disastrous.

Connor tunneled a hand through his mop of blond hair. "Maybe she'll come back."

Kyla shot a hard stare in his direction. "Are you willing to wait until the eleventh hour to see? I'm not. We all need to turn our efforts to tracking her down. She has to go down that aisle if I have to march her there in handcuffs myself."

GRAB your copy of *Cowboy in a Kilt* today!

OTHER BOOKS BY KAIT NOLAN

A complete and up-to-date list of all my books can be found at https://kaitnolan.com.

KILTED HEARTS
SMALL TOWN CONTEMPORARY SCOTTISH ROMANCE

- *Jilting The Kilt* (prequel)
- *Cowboy in a Kilt* (Raleigh and Kyla)
- *Grump in a Kilt* (Malcolm and Charlotte)
- *Playboy in a Kilt* (Connor and Sophie)
- *Protector in a Kilt* (Ewan and Isobel)
- *Single Dad in a Kilt* (Hamish and Afton)
- *Kilty Pleasures* (Jason and Skye)

SPECIAL OPS SCOTS
SMALL TOWN MILITARY SCOTTISH ROMANCE

- *One Fine Night* (prequel)
- *Before Highland Sunset* (Alex and Ciara) October 4th, 2024

Bad Boy Bakers
Small Town Military Romance

- *Rescued By a Bad Boy* (Brax and Mia prequel)
- *Mixed Up With a Marine* (Brax and Mia)
- *Wrapped Up with a Ranger* (Holt and Cayla)
- *Stirred Up by a SEAL* (Jonah and Rachel)
- *Hung Up on the Hacker* (Cash and Hadley)
- *Caught Up with the Captain* (Grey and Rebecca)

Rescue My Heart Series
Small Town Military Romance

- *Someone Like You* (Ivy and Harrison)
- *What I Like About You* (Laurel and Sebastian)
- *Bad Case of Loving You* (Paisley and Ty prequel) Included in *Made For Loving You* (Paisley and Ty)

The Misfit Inn Series
Small Town Family Romance

- *When You Got A Good Thing* (Kennedy and Xander)
- *Til There Was You* (Misty and Denver)
- *Those Sweet Words* (Pru and Flynn)
- *Stay A Little Longer* (Athena and Logan)
- *Bring It On Home* (Maggie and Porter)
- *Come Away with Me* (Moses and Zuri)

Men of The Misfit Inn
Small Town Southern Romance

- *Let It Be Me* (Emerson and Caleb)
- *Our Kind of Love* (Abbey and Kyle)
- *Don't You Wanna Stay* (Deanna and Wyatt)

- *Until We Meet Again* (Samantha and Griffin prequel)
- *Come A Little Closer* (Samantha and Griffin)
- *Just Wanted You To Know* (Livia and Declan)
- *A Love Like You* (Juliette and Mick)

Wishful Romance Series
Small Town Southern Romance

- *To Get Me To You* (Cam and Norah)
- *Know Me Well* (Liam and Riley)
- *Be Careful, It's My Heart* (Brody and Tyler)
- *The Matchmaker Maneuver* (Myles and Piper prequel)
- *Just For This Moment* (Myles and Piper)
- *Wish I Might* (Reed and Cecily)
- *Turn My World Around* (Tucker and Corinne)
- *Dance Me A Dream* (Jace and Tara)
- *See You Again* (Trey and Sandy)
- *The Christmas Fountain* (Chad and Mary Alice)
- *You Were Meant For Me* (Mitch and Tess)
- *A Lot Like Christmas* (Ryan and Hannah)
- *Dancing Away With My Heart* (Zach and Lexi)

Wishful Moments Series
Bite-Sized Wishful Romance

- *Once Upon A Coffee* (Avery and Dillon)
- *Once Upon A Rescue* (Brooke and Hayden)
- *Who I Am with You* (Dinah and Robert)

Wishing For a Hero Series (A Wishful Spinoff Series)
Small Town Romantic Suspense

- *Make You Feel My Love* (Judd and Autumn)
- *Watch Over Me* (Nash and Rowan)

- *Can't Take My Eyes Off You* (Ethan and Miranda)
- *Burn For You* (Sean and Delaney)

Meet Cute Romance
Small Town Short Romance

- *Once Upon A Snow Day*
- *Once Upon A New Year's Eve*
- *Once Upon An Heirloom*

Summer Fling Trilogy
Contemporary Romance

- *Second Chance Summer*
- *Summer Camp Secret*
- *The Summer Camp Swap*

ABOUT KAIT

Kait is a Mississippi native, who often swears like a sailor, calls everyone sugar, honey, or darlin', and can wield a bless your heart like a saber or a Snuggie, depending on requirements.

You can find more information on this *USA Today* best selling and RITA ® Award-winning author and her books on her website http://kaitnolan.com.

Do you need more small town sass and spark? Sign up for her newsletter to hear about new releases, book deals, and exclusive content!

Milton Keynes UK
Ingram Content Group UK Ltd.
UKHW020016130624
443988UK00021B/712